D0622769

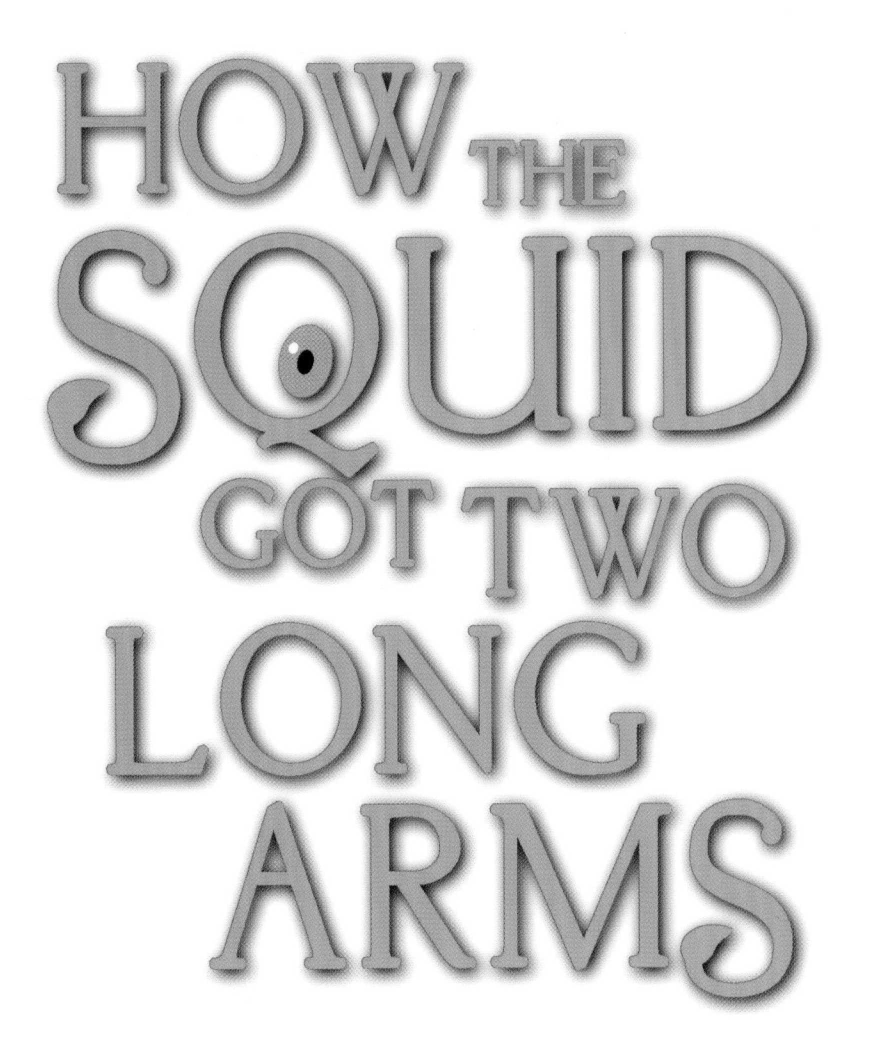

By Henry Herz
Art by Luke Graber

PELICAN PUBLISHING COMPANY
GRETNA 2018

**Library of Congress Cataloging-in-Publication Data**

Names: Herz, Henry, author. | Graber, Luke, illustrator.
Title: How the squid got two long arms / Henry Herz ; illustrated by Luke Graber.
Description: Gretna : Pelican Publishing Company, 2018. | Summary: A squid that feels cold begins stealing clothing from other animals until, finally, they fight back, leaving him with two arms longer than the others. Includes facts about squids.
Identifiers: LCCN 2018000420| ISBN 9781455623884 (hardcover : alk. paper) |
ISBN 9781455623891 (ebook)
Subjects: | CYAC: Squids—Fiction. | Stealing—Fiction. | Clothing and dress—Fiction. | Greed—Fiction. | Marine animals—Fiction.
Classification: LCC PZ7.1.H4955 How 2018 | DDC [E]—dc23 LC record available at https://lccn.loc.gov/2018000420

Printed in Malaysia
Published by Pelican Publishing Company, Inc.
1000 Burmaster Street, Gretna, Louisiana 70053
www.pelicanpub.com

*With thanks to*
*Jon Klassen, Rudyard Kipling,*
*and the Author of all things*

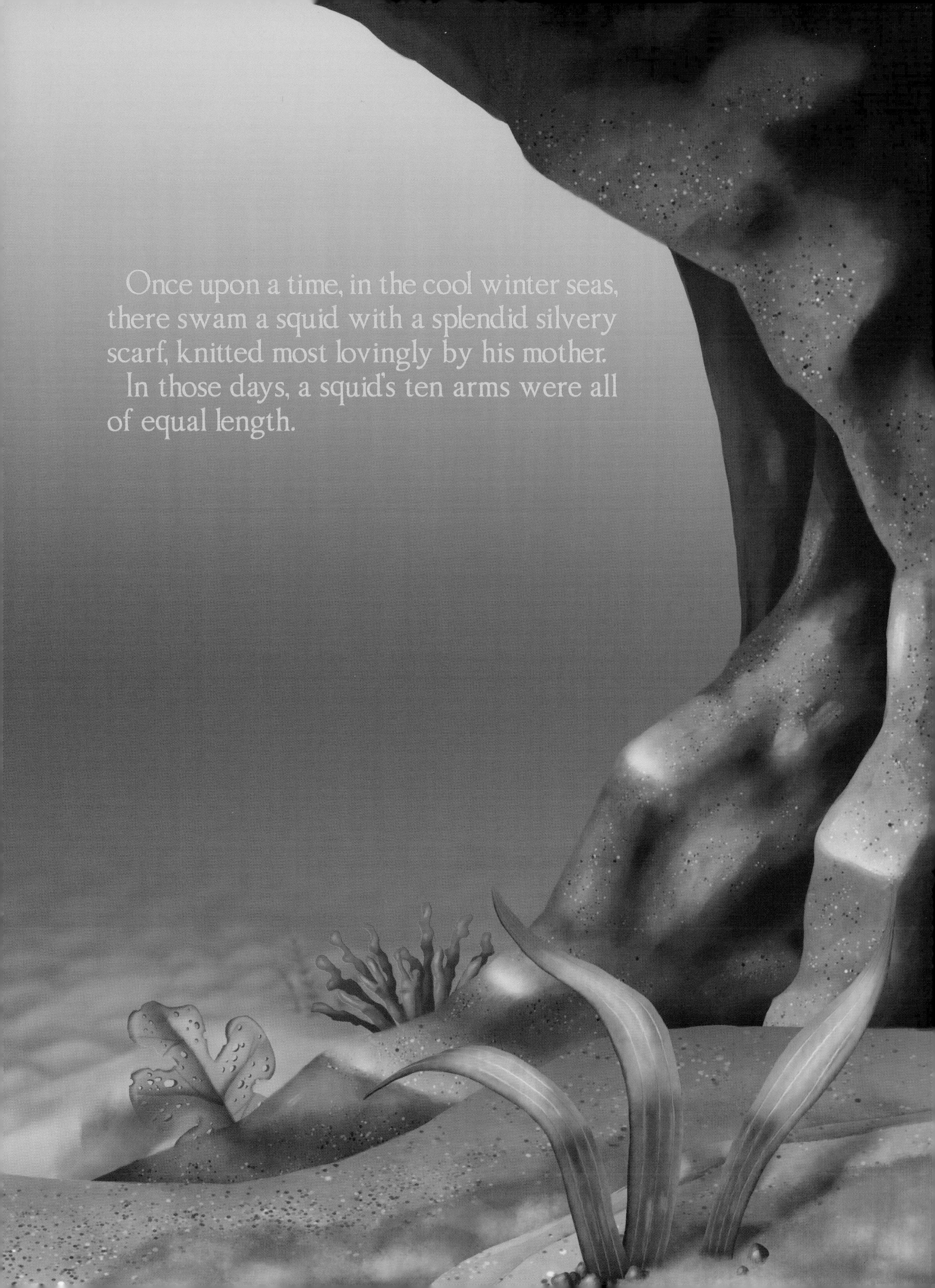

Once upon a time, in the cool winter seas, there swam a squid with a splendid silvery scarf, knitted most lovingly by his mother.

In those days, a squid's ten arms were all of equal length.

Although the squid's scarf shimmered like sunlight on the sea's surface, it did little to keep him warm. Shivering, he swiped an octopus's sweater during her noontime nap.

The sweater, while stylish and soft, sported only eight sleeves.

Still, eight sleeves are better than none, 'tis said.

Not yet warm, the squid swam off to steal more clothes.

He squirted a billowy ink cloud to prevent pursuit by the offended octopus.

Searching left and right and left again, the squid spied a fiddler crab strolling on the seafloor, collecting whatever morsels and tidbits such crabs fancy.

The squid swooped in, swiping the crab's mitten with little difficulty, and even less guilt.

Still cold, the squid continued his quest for clothes, confident that the creeping crab couldn't catch him.

Gliding past some seaweed and over a reef, the squid spotted an eel wearing a cap. But not just any cap—a spectacular cap, wondrous and warm, the likes of which he'd never before beheld. The cap's color even matched his sweater!

The eel withdrew into his cave.
The squid's greed grew and grew
until it grabbed him like a riptide.

The squid *reached* in to snatch the cap. . . .

The eel *nabbed* one arm.

The crab *grabbed* another. . . .

Their stolen items recovered, the octopus and crab went on their way.

The squid was left only with his splendid silvery scarf, the realization that he was no warmer despite all his piracy, and a pair of arms noticeably longer than the others.

# AUTHOR'S NOTE

Squid are amazing animals, just like their fellow cephalopods, octopuses and cuttlefish. Like them, squid can squirt ink to distract any attackers.

Squid are shaped roughly like octopuses, but in addition to eight arms, squid also have two longer tentacles. Imagine how well you could play basketball with ten arms!

Most squid are no more than two feet long, but giant squid can grow to over forty feet. Squid have cone-shaped mantles. The mantle's fins help them steer. Squid blow water out of their siphons to move—jet propulsion!